CONTENTS

Jamie waved goodbye to his mum,
shoved his lunchbox into his backpack,
and charged out of the lighthouse where
they lived. He was meeting his best
friend, Tess, in Ammonite Bay to search
for fossils.

He scrambled down the steep path
to the beach. Tess was already there,
scrabbling around in a patch of pebbles.

'Found one!' Tess's freckly face,

4

'Hey, what's that?' Asked Tess.

A low boom was echoing over the jungle. The note rose higher as the sound got louder and louder.

Whooop, whooo-ooop, whooo-ooo-ooop!

There was an answering call.

Wheeep, wheee-eeep, wheee-eee-eeep!

13

Tess giggled. 'The first one sounds like you trying to play the trumpet.'

'The second one's more like a giant guinea pig with a megaphone.' Jamie laughed. 'Can't wait to see the dinosaurs that are making that noise!'

They slithered down the steep fern-covered slope, into the jungle. Jamie skidded to a halt beside a huge rotting tree trunk, covered in moss. A frilly purple fungus shaped like a half-moon sprouted from the side. It was crumpled, and smelled of garlic.

Tess knocked on the trunk. 'It's hollow – the inside must have rotted away.'

Grunk!

A small, scaly, green-brown
dinosaur with a flat bony head jumped
out at them. Jamie fell over backwards
with surprise.

Grunk, grunk, grunk! The dino
nudged him with his bony head.

'We're happy to see you too, Wanna!'
Jamie scratched the top of the little
dinosaur's head. His skin felt like
sandpaper and he stank of ginkgo
fruit – and garlic. There was a purple
patch on his side.

'Why have you been rubbing yourself on that purple fungus?' Tess wondered, as she scratched him under his chin.

Suddenly, Wanna froze. Jamie and Tess looked at each other. Branches were snapping and ferns were rustling. Something was crashing through the jungle towards them – and it was fast!

Wanna dived head-first into the rotting tree trunk. Tess and Jamie squeezed in beside him. Just in time…

From their hiding place, they glimpsed a massive head parting the ferns. Its huge jaws were lined with long, pointed teeth, their edges serrated like knives.

'Wow!' Jamie gasped. 'A T. rex!'

'So cool!' Tess breathed. She wanted to present nature shows on TV when she grew up. 'Tyrannosaurus rex is the deadliest meat-eater ever,' she whispered, in her best TV presenter voice. 'It has around 60 fearsome teeth, like steel bananas, with edges like hacksaws which curve backward into those huge jaws. If a T. rex gets hold of you, it's never going to let you go.'

Jamie gulped.

'It's the perfect predator,' Tess went on. 'Look at its huge yellow eyes. They can easily spot prey. The pupils are narrowing to slits, like a cat's. That must help it see in the dark!'

'And focus on its prey…' Jamie said in a low voice. Beside him, he could feel Wanna shaking.

The T. rex sniffed deeply. **Snuuuuurf!**
'Palaeontologists think T. rex had the best sense of smell of any dino yet discovered,' Tess said in awe.

'Er, Tess,' Jamie said. 'I think it kn-kn-knows we're here...'

The ground shook as the T. rex leaped out of the ferns. It stood perfectly balanced on two enormous legs. Its huge feet looked like bigger versions of an ostrich's. All down its back, to the tip of its tail, it had faint reddish tiger stripes that rippled and glowed in the Cretaceous sunshine.

'It's beautiful!' Tess breathed.

'It's deadly!' Jamie reminded her.

Snuuurf! The T. rex sniffed again and took a step in their direction.

On the Trail of a T. rex

Written by Rex Stone Illustrated by Louise Forshaw

This book belongs to:

....

I am a reader and I celebrated World Book Day 2024
with this gift from my local bookseller and DK Books.

WORLD BOOK DAY®

World Book Day's mission is to offer every child and young person
the opportunity to read and love books by giving you
the chance to have a book of your own.

To find out more, and for fun activities including video stories,
audiobooks and book recommendations, visit worldbookday.com

World Book Day is a charity sponsored by National Book Tokens.

Jamie has just moved to Ammonite Bay, a stretch of coastline famed for its fossils. Jamie is a member of Dinosaur Club – a network of kids who share dinosaur knowledge, help identify fossils, post new discoveries, and chat about all things prehistoric. Jamie carries his tablet everywhere in case he needs to contact the Club.

Jamie is exploring Ammonite Bay when he meets Tess, another member of Dinosaur Club. Tess takes Jamie to a cave with a strange tunnel and some dinosaur footprints. When they walk along the footprints, the two new friends find themselves back in the time of the dinosaurs!

It's amazing, but dangerous too – and they'll definitely need help from Dinosaur Club…

'This tree trunk isn't strong enough to protect us,' Jamie said. 'We'll be dino dinner!'

RrrrrrrRrrrrrRrrrr, the T. rex rumbled. Jamie could feel the vibrations going through his body. Wanna shivered.

The enormous predator bent its gigantic head over the tree trunk.

'T…T….T…rex has very bad breath,' Tess stammered.

Jamie closed his eyes.

RrrrrrrRrrrrrRrrrr! The T. rex shook its head and backed away from the tree trunk. Then it reared up, swishing its tail violently from side to side. It stalked off through the jungle, still swinging its tail. Its crashing and smashing echoed through the trees.

Jamie sighed with relief.

'I can't believe it didn't break open the tree trunk with its claws and eat us. Its arms are short, but still long enough for that.' Tess sounded puzzled.

Jamie pointed to the frill of purple fungus. 'I don't think it likes the smell of garlic.'

'That must be it.' Tess crawled out of the tree trunk. 'I wonder, why it was thrashing its tail so much?

Maybe something is wrong. Let's follow it and find out.'

'Okay,' Jamie agreed, brushing leaf mould off his jeans. 'From a safe distance, though...'

Grunk! Wanna fell into line behind Jamie and Tess.

They followed the trail of crushed ferns and broken tree branches.

'It's easy to track a T. rex!' Tess said.

The trail opened out. They could see the colossal predator lashing its tail at the trunk of a small conifer tree on the side of a clearing. Jamie, Tess, and Wanna watched from behind a clump of ferns. *Smash!* The conifer fell to the ground.

The T. rex backed towards another tree and lashed out again with its tail.

Crash! Another young conifer fell. Wanna hid behind Jamie.

'Strange…' Jamie murmured. 'It's almost like it hates trees.'

'More like it hates its tail…' Tess stared through her binoculars. 'I can see something sticking out at the end of it. Maybe a stick from all the thrashing about.' Tess handed the binoculars to Jamie.

Jamie steadied the binoculars on Tess's shoulder.

'It looks too pale to be a stick…'

The giant reptile turned and lumbered off. Tess grabbed the binoculars and focused on the tip of its tail as it disappeared into the Cretaceous jungle. She gasped.

There was another flash, and Tess appeared beside him. She screwed up her face. 'Eww. Smells like sick!'

Jamie pointed to some trees with yellowy-green, fan-shaped leaves. 'It's because the ginkgo trees are dropping their stinky fruit.'

'Wanna will be happy.' Tess grinned. Their little dinosaur friend loved ginkgo fruit. 'I can't wait to see him again!'

They squelched through pools of rotting fruit to the top of a hill. From there, they had a great view over a dense green jungle of tree ferns, cycads, and conifers. Beyond lay dusty plains and a lagoon. In the distance were mountains and the shimmer of the ocean.

'The Cretaceous!' Jamie and Tess jumped for joy as they high-fived.

A faint Aq-qqq-qqqqrk cut through the constant hum of insects.

Tess wiped her binoculars on her T-shirt and put them to her eyes. 'Look! There's a gigantic pterosaur flying over the lagoon!'

She passed the binoculars to Jamie. He watched the winged creature swoop down to the water in search of prey. 'So cool!'

'It's not a stick, it's a T. rex tooth,' she said. 'This dino must've been fighting with another T. rex over food or territory, and got bitten.'

'Owww!' said Jamie. 'That's got to hurt!'

'Poor T. rex!' Tess exclaimed. 'It's just trying to get the tooth out of its tail. We have to help it.'

CHAPTER 3

The trail led them into a tangle of ferns and cycads. Soon, they heard the sound of rushing water.

Jamie and Tess peeped through a gap in the fern fronds. The T. rex was standing in the middle of the river, swishing its tail through the water.

'That must be helping the pain,' Tess whispered.

'Jurassic or Cretaceous?' Asked Jamie.

 'Cretaceous.' The reply came from Kim, who lived in Korea.

 'Late Cretaceous,' added Leon from Germany. 'Around 66 million years ago.'

Tess leaned over to type a reply. 'Great!'

Jamie carefully stored the ammonite and the tablet in his backpack and grinned at Tess. Finding fossils was fun, but Jamie and Tess had discovered something even better: a world of living, breathing dinosaurs! This Cretaceous fossil was going to help them travel to the *actual* Cretaceous period for an exciting adventure.

'Race you there!' Tess's boots kicked up a spray of sand and pebbles as she sped off towards the opposite end of the bay. The two friends climbed up the boulders and dashed to the entrance of the old smugglers cave.

Jamie clicked on his torch and ran the beam of light along the back wall of the cave, until it disappeared into a narrow gap in the rocks. He watched Tess squeeze through the gap, then took a deep breath, and followed.

The second cave was their special secret. It was eerily silent, dark, and damp – and it had five fossil dinosaur footprints embedded in the floor.

Jamie stepped onto the first footprint. He began to count as he walked along the ancient dino tracks.

'One, two, three…'

His whole body buzzed
with excitement.

'Four…

Five…'

There was a dazzling *flash* of light.

Instantly, Jamie was outside in bright daylight. A dragonfly the size of a paper aeroplane whizzed past his nose, and his ears rang with the high-pitched whirring noise of countless insects.

Jamie breathed in the warm humid air. Yuck! Something here smelled worse than Granddad's compost heap on a hot summer day. He glanced down. He was standing in a puddle of orange slime covered in a fuzzy pinkish mould. There were small dinosaur footprints all over it.

Tess got onto her stomach and began
to crawl with her elbows towards the
cycad. Once she was behind the trunk
she got up into a crouch and gave Jamie
and Wanna a thumbs-up.

Jamie flattened himself on the soft,
compost-like ground. Wanna cowered
beside him.

'It's okay to be frightened,' Jamie told
him. 'I know the T. rex is scary!'

Jamie and Wanna hauled themselves to the cycad and crouched down beside Tess. All three were splattered with dino snot, mud, and pine needles, and Jamie and Tess had bits of fern stuck in their hair.

'Now all we have do is–' Before Tess could finish her sentence, the huge predator stepped out of the river and shook itself from head to tail, showering them with water droplets. It turned its back to them and swung its tail.

'Watch out!' Tess yelled. The three friends flattened themselves among a clump of ferns as…

Thrash! The T. rex's tail uprooted the cycad and catapulted it into the stream.

'That was close,' Jamie gasped,
as the T. rex stalked off again.
'Wait. Where's Wanna?'

'He shot off behind those rocks.' Tess pointed in the opposite direction to the way the T. rex had gone. 'Let's make sure that he's okay.'

They found Wanna sheltering under two rocks that leaned together like a tent, happily munching on a ginkgo that had dropped from a nearby tree. He greeted them with a gentle head bump.

Jamie smiled. 'Yes, I'm hungry too,'

'Let's have our lunch,' said Tess. 'We can think up a new plan to pull out that tooth while we eat.'

They squeezed in beside Wanna and Jamie took out his lunch box. 'Yum! Leftover garlic bread' he said, giving a piece to Tess. He offered one to Wanna, but the little dinosaur made a gakking noise and shook his head. Jamie laughed. 'He doesn't mind the smell of garlic, but he doesn't like the taste.'

'Let's ask Dinosaur Club for help,'
Tess mumbled through a mouthful of
cold garlic bread.

Jamie took out his tablet. He tapped
on the app and opened the chat box.

'How do you pull a tooth out of
the tail of a T. rex?' He wrote.

The responses came in right away.

'How are we going to get close
enough to pull out the tooth?'
Jamie asked quietly.

'See that cycad on the river bank?'
Tess pointed to a big plant with a
barrel-shaped trunk, sprouting a crown
of fern-like leaves. 'We can hide behind
it. Then when the T. rex's tail is close
enough, I'll jump out and grab the tooth.
Stay low so it doesn't see us!'

crocodile T-shirt, and binoculars were splattered with mud and sand. She held up a round fossil the size of a bottle top. It looked like a coil of grey modelling clay, but it had once been a sea creature with tentacles and a shell.

'Cool!' Jamie dumped his backpack beside Tess and took out the tablet that went everywhere with him. *Click!* He snapped a photo of the ammonite, then pressed the dino footprint icon to open the app for Dinosaur Club. He posted the photo, and immediately messages popped up from kids that lived all over the world, who loved dinosaurs and fossils as much as he and Tess did.

'Nice ammonite!' Commented Laura, from the Netherlands.

6

'You need to distract it, then get up close,' said Chloe from the USA.

 'How?' Asked Tess.

'Pretend to be prey,' suggested Angelo, who was from the Philippines.

Jamie looked at Tess. 'But how do we pretend to be prey without ending up getting eaten?'

Tess thought hard. 'We need to be in a safe hiding place,' she said, 'then attract it to us.' She held up the rest of her garlic bread. 'But we all smell of garlic now, so it won't like our scent. Maybe a noise will make it come closer?'

Jamie nodded. 'Remember that trumpeting noise we heard when we arrived? I wonder if T. rex hunted the dinosaur that made that sound?'

'Let's ask the club.'

Jamie typed in the chat box. 'What dino made a trumpeting noise?'

A response flashed up. 'A duck-billed dino called Parasaurolophus,' said Tamiko from Japan.

She sent a picture, too.

'They used the long hollow crests on their heads to make the sound.'

'Did T. rex hunt Parasaurolophus?' Jamie asked.

'Yep,' came Tamiko's reply.

Jamie typed in a thank you and closed the app.

'Great!' said Tess. 'Now we can make a plan...'

'I'll climb up a tree and make a noise like Parasaurolophus.' Jamie chose a conifer with a red trunk. It looked more difficult to climb than the ginkgo tree next to it, but it was sturdy enough to withstand the lash of a T. rex tail.

'I'll hide in the ferns over there, then leap out and pull out the tooth,' Tess said.

'Let's wrap our hands in fern fronds to protect them from any sharp edges,' Jamie suggested.

Grunk? It sounded like a question.

'You stay here!' Jamie and Tess told Wanna together.

Jamie hauled himself from branch to branch, scattering pine needles and cones as he climbed. When he reached the top, he discarded his fern fronds and sat with his back to the trunk of the tree, with his legs dangling either side of a branch.

'Ready?' He called.

In response, Tess's leaf-wrapped hand emerged from a clump of ferns, and gave him a thumbs-up.

Jamie cupped his hands around his mouth.

Whooop! Whooo-ooop! Whooo-oooo-oop! He trumpeted again and again and again. It was hard work making a sound like a Parasaurolophus. *It must be easier if you have a crest to echo your call!* Jamie thought, while gasping for breath.

Soon he could hear the unmistakable sounds of the T. rex crashing through the jungle. It was coming towards them. Would their plan work? Were his feet within range of a snappy T. rex?

Jamie stood up on the branch.
His heart was thumping and his knees
were wobbling. Would they all make it
out of this alive?

CHAPTER 4

Hidden in the ferns, Tess was trembling from head to toe. She wasn't sure whether it was because she was excited or terrified — or a little of both. The T. rex was slowly circling Jamie's tree, trying to find the Parasaurolophus. Their plan was working!

RrrrRrrrRrrr, it rumbled.

Whooop! Whooo-ooop!

Jamie trumpeted. The T. rex peered
into the tree.

Tess creeped closer. She was so close now, she could see the powerful muscles rippling beneath the predator's scaly skin. The feathery quills on the great dino's legs quivered as it lowered its tail to the ground and stretched its neck so its head was high up in Jamie's tree.

Snuurf! She could hear it sniffing.

This was her only chance. Tess checked the leaves were wrapped tightly around her hands. She took a deep breath, rushed out of her hiding place, and grabbed the tooth. She pulled with all her might. With a sudden pop, the tooth came away. Tess lost her grip and the tooth soared into the air

Splash! It landed in the river.

Raaar! The T. rex roared in surprise
and whirled round. But Tess had already
climbed the tree. She ripped the leaves
from her hands and scaled the branches
as fast as she could. At the top of the tree,
she was level with Jamie. The branch he
was standing on was almost touching
hers. She put her fingers to her lips.

Beneath them, the T. rex was still twisting around. It twitched its tail, and peered at the end of it, as if it was puzzled by what had happened. Then it straightened up and gave another sniff. Tess and Jamie held their breath, but it wasn't interested in them. The T. rex shook its head, stuck out its tail, and stomped off into the ferns. For a minute or two, they could still hear it rumbling to itself. But now, the rumbles sounded like giant contented purrs.

'We did it!' Tess and Jamie high-fived across the treetops.

Below, Wanna's nose poked out from the rock tent. Tess plucked a handful of sticky, stinky ginkgoes and threw them down for him. Wanna gave a happy **grunk**. He raced out from his hiding place and began to gobble them up.

From high in the trees, Jamie and Tess turned to look out over the plains that lay beyond the jungle. They could see a herd of armour-plated ankylosaurs trundling slowly past some rocks. Suddenly, the T. rex emerged from the trees.

Whoooooop!
Wheeeeeeeeeeeep!

A pair of Parasaurolophus trumpeted in alarm and raced away from it in a cloud of dust.

Aaark, aaark, aaaark! The call was so close it was almost deafening. Jamie and Tess ducked as a pterosaur the size of a plane soared overhead. 'Quetzalcoatlus!' Tess gasped.

They watched the winged reptile disappear into the distance.

'Wow!' Jamie grinned from ear to ear. 'The Cretaceous is amazing!'

'It is!' Tess's smile lit up her freckly face. 'And we can come back whenever we like. Or we can go to the Jurassic period, or the Triassic… I wonder what our next adventure will be?'

'Whatever it is,' Jamie said, 'I can't wait to share it with Dinosaur Club!'

Dinosaur timeline

The Triassic
(250-200 million years ago)

The first period of the Mesozoic Era was the Triassic.
During the Triassic, there were very few plants, and
the Earth was hot and dry, like a desert. Most of the
dinosaurs that lived during the Triassic were small.

The Jurassic
(200-145 million years ago)

The second period of the Mesozoic Era was the Jurassic.
During the Jurassic, the Earth became cooler and wetter,
which caused lots of plants to grow. This created lots of
food for dinosaurs that helped them grow big and thrive.

The Cretaceous
(145-66 million years ago)

The third and final period of the Mesozoic Era was the
Cretaceous. During the Cretaceous, dinosaurs were at
their peak and dominated the Earth, but at the end
most of them suddenly became extinct.

Dinosaurs existed during a time on Earth known as the Mesozoic Era. It lasted for more than 180 million years, and was split into three different periods: the Triassic, Jurassic, and the Cretaceous.

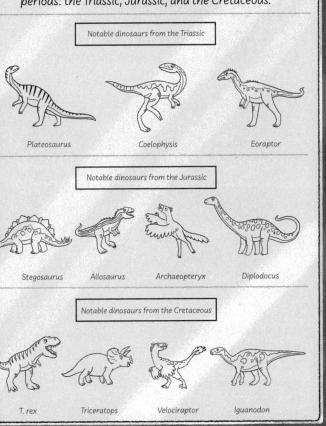

Notable dinosaurs from the Triassic

Plateosaurus   Coelophysis   Eoraptor

Notable dinosaurs from the Jurassic

Stegosaurus   Allosaurus   Archaeopteryx   Diplodocus

Notable dinosaurs from the Cretaceous

T. rex   Triceratops   Velociraptor   Iguanodon

DINO DATA

Also known as T. rex, Tyrannosaurus was the most powerful and dangerous land predator of all time. It is sometimes called "King of the Dinosaurs".

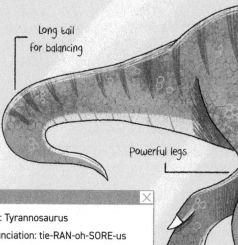

Long tail for balancing

Powerful legs

Name: Tyrannosaurus
Pronunciation: tie-RAN-oh-SORE-us
Period: Cretaceous
Size: 12m (39ft) long
Habitat: Forests and swamps
Diet: Meat

Huge head

Sharp teeth

Small arms

FACT

The name Tyrannosaurus means "tyrant lizard".

61

DINO DATA

Wannanosaurus was a small dinosaur from the late Cretaceous period. It is known for having a very hard skull.

Bristles

Name: Wannanosaurus

Pronunciation: wah-NON-oh-SORE-us

Period: Cretaceous

Size: 60cm (2ft) long

Habitat: Woodlands

Diet: Plants, fruit, seeds

FACT

Wannanosaurus fossils were discovered in China.

Hard skull

FACT

Scientists aren't sure whether Wannanosaurus used its skull to defend itself from predators or to fight off rivals.

GLOSSARY

AMMONITE
A type of sea creature that lived during
the time of the dinosaurs

CARNIVORE
An animal that only eats meat

CRETACEOUS
The third period of the time dinosaurs
existed (145-66 million years ago)

CYCAD
A type of plant that dates back
millions of years

DINOSAUR
A group of ancient reptiles that lived
millions of years ago

FOSSIL
Remains of a living thing that have become preserved over time

GINKGO
A type of tree that dates back millions of years

HERBIVORE
An animal that only eats plant matter

PALAEONTOLOGIST
A scientist who studies dinosaurs and other fossils

PTEROSAUR
Ancient flying reptiles that existed at the same time as dinosaurs

REPTILE
A group of scaly, cold-blooded animals that includes lizards, crocodiles, snakes, and dinosaurs

DO YOU HAVE WHAT IT TAKES TO JOIN THE DINOSAUR CLUB?

The T. rex Attack

A Triceratops Charge

Saving the Stegosaurus

The Compsognathus Chase

Catching the Velociraptor

Escaping the Liopleurodon

Avoiding the Allosaurus

Flight of the Quetzalcoatlus

March of the Ankylosaurus

READ ON FOR AN EXTRACT OF

Tracking the Diplodocus

From his tree, Jamie could see the
diplodocus shaking his head wildly
from side to side. Any minute now, Tess
would fall off or be crushed against a
tree trunk. He had to save his friend!

The end of a thick creeper dangled
before his eyes. Jamie took a deep breath,
grabbed onto the vine and launched
himself towards the next tree. He swung

safely across to a thick branch with more vines hanging down. He took hold and leapt off, swinging from tree to tree through the jungle after Tess.

Beneath him, Wanna was leaping logs and dodging branches in his struggle to keep up.

'Yee-haw!' Jamie called as he swung, and soon he swung around so he was next to the lumbering diplodocus. Tess was just below the dinosaur's head, and was clinging on for dear life.

'Help!' Tess shouted at the top of her lungs. 'I can't hold on much longer!'

'I'll get you,' Jamie shouted back. He launched himself onto another vine and swung across the diplodocus's path. 'Grab my hand!'

Their fingertips brushed as Jamie swung past the dinosaur's eyes, but he wasn't close enough to reach Tess.

The diplodocus stopped thrashing his head and looked in surprise as Jamie swung back onto the tree.

'I'm coming again!' Jamie took a deep breath and launched himself from the same vine. He swung towards Tess, rising higher and higher, right above the dino's head! At the top of the swing, he stretched his hand down to Tess.

Tess reached up, and they interlocked their fingers.

Jamie had done it!

Snap! The vine gave way.

Jamie plummeted down, and was only saved by his friend's firm grip. While Tess held onto the diplodocus's neck with all her might, Jamie pulled himself up towards the giant reptile's scaly head and clawed for a handhold. He grabbed what felt like a slimy rubbery ledge. He was dangling from the diplodocus's spitty bottom lip!

Whoooooo!

The diplodocus dropped his head and Jamie quickly let go and tumbled to the ground. Tess landed in a heap beside him.

As the diplodocus pulled away, Jamie could see a piece of wood the size of a baseball bat lodged between the dinosaur's brown teeth and rubbery gums.

'That was awesome!' Tess gasped, checking that her binoculars were in one piece. 'I've never swung from a dinosaur before.'

'First time for me, too,' Jamie panted, trying to catch his breath as he untangled himself from his backpack.

Wanna hurtled out of the jungle and leapt on them, grunking enthusiastically.

'Get off, we're okay!' Jamie struggled to his feet.

Whooooooo!

The diplodocus was wailing again, scraping his jaws along the ground. Then he lifted his head and shook it from side to side.

'I know what's making him so crazy,' Jamie told Tess. 'I saw a piece of tree branch stuck between his teeth.'

As they watched the huge dinosaur stomp off again, Tess said, 'Poor Dippy's got toothache.'

Jamie nodded. 'I had toothache once and it really hurt.'

'We need a dinosaur dentist,' Tess said, 'but we can't just call one up.'

They looked at each
other and grinned.

'Let's go after him,' Jamie said.

Tess nodded. 'We'll be
Dippy's dentists!'

Happy
World Book Day!

When you've read this book, you can keep the fun going by swapping it, talking about it with a friend, or reading it again!

What do you want to read next? Whether it's **comics**, **audiobooks**, **recipe books** or **non-fiction** you can visit your school, local library or nearest bookshop for your next read – someone will always be happy to help.